Rock 'n' Roll Moles

By Samantha Montgomerie

Illustrated by Carissa Harris

Chapter 1

Digby yawned. It had been another late night of digging. Now it was time for bed. It would not be long before morning, when he and his friends would start digging all over again.

Rock 'n' Roll Moles

'Samantha Montgomerie'

An original concept by Samantha Montgomerie

© Samantha Montgomerie 2025

Illustrated by Carissa Harris

Published by MAVERICK ARTS PUBLISHING LTD

Suite 1, Hillreed House, 54 Queen Street,

Horsham, West Sussex, RH13 5AD

© Maverick Arts Publishing Limited August 2025

+44 (0)1403 256941

A CIP catalogue record for this book is available at the British Library.

ISBN 978-1-83511-076-8

Printed in India

Maverick
publishing

www.maverickbooks.co.uk

Gold

This book is rated as: Gold Band (Guided Reading)

They were building Mudwiggle Mansion, the biggest mole burrow ever built. With its long tunnels and food storage areas, it would be the perfect mansion for moles—out of the sunlight with plenty of tasty worms and insects to feast on. A quiet hideaway.

"Goodnight," said Mudsy. "See you in the morning."

"Goodnight," said Digby.

Digby slipped into the quiet of his room. He curled up in his bed and listened to the gentle snores echoing in the silent tunnels. Digby waited. But he wasn't waiting to go to sleep. He was waiting and listening for something to begin.

A loud beat trembled through the ground. Digby heard the crash of drums. He felt the thrum of an electric guitar. The speakers in the human house above his room boomed out a rock 'n' roll song.

Digby's feet tapped in time. He loved how the beat boomed and quivered around him. He loved how the music was loud and alive. Digby grinned as the music trembled all around.

Digby slipped out of bed. He grabbed his bag and put in a pencil, a notepad and his jar of glow worms. Then he crept out, tiptoeing past his snoring friends. They were so used to the noise that they slept through it.

At the far end of the tunnel, Digby started to dig. He moved his arms hard and fast, digging deeper and deeper down.

Soon he had finished digging a small den in the earth.

"This is perfect," said Digby.

By the golden light of the glow worms, Digby began to write. He tapped his feet as a beat came into his head. He scribbled down words to match the beat. Digby wrote and wrote as the song swirled in his head and out onto the page.

When he had finished, Digby cleared his throat and sang his song.

"I love mud, and I love moles,
so tap your feet to the beat."

He tapped his feet, imagining the crash of drums and the thrum of a guitar. Digby let his voice boom as he sang in his secret den.

Chapter 2

It would soon be time for the moles to start their morning digging. Digby scurried back to his room, and the hush of Mudwiggle Mansion surrounded him again.

"What would the others think of my rowdy song?" thought Digby. He blushed. There was not much that was 'rock 'n' roll' about mole life.

As he lay in bed, Digby imagined singing his song on stage. It would be loud enough to make the ground tremble. It would fill all the tunnels with its thumping beats. His band would play, wearing rockstar quiffs and leather jackets. They would be a rock sensation!

As he drifted off to sleep, Digby knew he wanted to be a rock 'n' roll mole, no matter what.

Digby woke to a banging on his door.

"Digby, wake up!" called Mudsy. "It's time
to dig."

He slowly rubbed the sleep out of his eyes as
he dragged himself out of bed.

Digby joined the line of moles shuffling down the tunnel.

Scrape, dig. Scrape, dig. They dug quickly and quietly. Digby's mind started to wander. He felt the beats of his song fill his head. As he scooped the dirt, he tapped his feet in time.

Digby peered back at Mudsy. She was tapping along! Digby tapped faster, thumping his feet into the earth. Mudsy thumped in time behind him.

"Cool," whispered Mudsy. "I like that beat, Digby. Being a mole is a bit too quiet. Sometimes I just want to sing!"

Digby stopped digging. Could Mudsy feel the same way?

"Your tapping is putting me off!" said Roz.

"Keep digging!" said Rick.

"Meet me at midnight under the oak tree," Digby whispered to Mudsy. "I have something to show you."

Chapter 3

The moonlight shone in honey-coloured
beams through the leaves of the oak tree.
"I want to play rock music," said Digby.
"And I can see you love music too, Mudsy.
Why don't we be the first rock 'n' roll moles?"

Mudsy smiled and nodded. "Wait here! I have
something to show you," said Mudsy.
She came back with a large bag and pulled
out a guitar. Digby grinned.

"Let's rock!" said Digby.

He sang Mudsy his song.

The moon beamed like a spotlight on Digby and Mudsy. Mudsy's claws flew over the guitar strings. The music rippled through the silence of the night. Digby nodded his head in time to the beat as he sang along.

Suddenly, Digby spotted movement in the shadows. It was Roz and Rick.

Digby's stomach knotted inside. "What if they report us?" he thought. Digby didn't think the quiet moles of Mudwiggle Mansion would approve of their loud music.

Chapter 4

The next night, Roz was waiting outside Digby's door.

"Your music has grown on Rick and me," she said. "Follow me."

Digby and Mudsy crept down the tunnel. Roz's burrow went deep into the earth. Outside her den, Digby could hear the crashing of drums. The beat made the ground tremble.

Inside, Rick banged a beat on the drums. Roz nodded her head in time and started to sing. Her voice echoed around the burrow. It was perfect for a rock band.

"Let's rock!" cried Digby.

Every night that week, when the moles of Mudwiggle Mansion slipped silently to sleep, the Rock 'n' Roll Moles rocked. Before long, they had perfected every note.

"I think we're ready," said Rick.

"It's time to show the other moles what we can do!" cried Roz.

"Every good rock band needs an audience," Mudsy cheered.

Digby's stomach did a funny flip inside. What if the quiet moles of Mudwiggle Mansion didn't agree?

Digby, Mudsy, Rick and Roz spent the next few nights digging.

They dug deep.
They dug wide.
A huge cavern opened out into the earth.
Mudsy placed glow worms around the roof of the cavern. It basked in the golden glow.
Roz lined the tunnels with their lights, which shone like stars leading the way.

"It's time to get ready," said Roz.

The moles pulled on their leather jackets, slipped on their dark shades and slicked their fur into quiffs.

"Let's rock!" said Mudsy.

Chapter 5

The crash of drums thrashed in the air.
The guitar twanged. The ground trembled
as their song filled the cavern

"I love mud, and I love moles, so tap your
feet to the beat," sang Digby and Roz.
Their quiffs bobbed in time to the beat.

The moles of Mudwiggle Mansion stomped and danced. They bobbed and bounced to the beat. Digby grinned. Following the beat in his heart had been a good thing after all. Mudwiggle Mansion was now perfect!

"Rock 'n' Roll Moles, rock on!" cried Digby.

The End

Book Bands for Guided Reading

The Institute of Education book banding system is a scale of colours that reflects the various levels of reading difficulty. The bands are assigned by taking into account the content, the language style, the layout and phonics. Word, phrase and sentence level work is also taken into consideration.

Maverick Early Readers are a bright, attractive range of books covering the pink to white bands. All of these books have been book banded for guided reading to the industry standard and edited by a leading educational consultant.

Pink
Red
Yellow
Blue
Green
Orange
Turquoise
Purple
Gold
White

Cool Duck and Lots of Hats
Catch It, Jess! and Cat Nap
The Space Race
Pirates Don't Drive Diggers
A Right Royal Mess

To view the whole Maverick Readers scheme, visit our website at
www.maverickearlyreaders.com

Or scan the QR code above to view our scheme instantly!